CONTENTS

CU00865603

The 3 Legged Race

Two Centipedes decided one day
To enter a Three Legged race!
With their back legs
at the ready,
They tied two front feet
with a lace

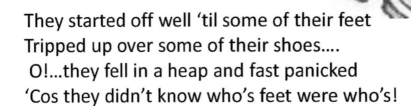

They started off well 'til some of their feet
Tripped up over some of their shoes....
O!...they fell in a heap and fast panicked
'Cos they didn't know who's feet were who's!

1

The solution arrived in the form of a Crab
Who offered to nip diverse toes
And whoever yelled out
the other would know
That the foot wasn't his, (I suppose)

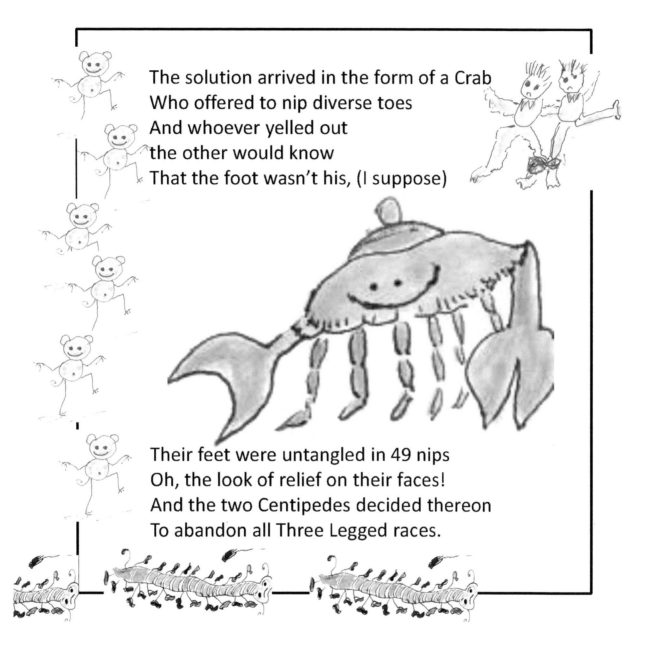

Their feet were untangled in 49 nips
Oh, the look of relief on their faces!
And the two Centipedes decided thereon
To abandon all Three Legged races.

2

A Cat's a Cat...

Two Fisher Mice
set sail one day,
To trawl the Catfish Creek

They aimed to goad
The swimming Cats
By calling them a "freak"

Well... they taunted
the wrong Catfish...
Who, smarting at the joke,
Looked hard at the Fisher Mice
Then overturned their boat.

Butterflies' Holiday

In the cold, cold winter, in the snow and ice. Brrr!
Do you ever wonder... where are the butterflies?
You'd be surprised!

Oh, they jet away to China, they live a life of ease
They loll about in deck chairs...
...eating pink ice creams. Yummy!

Yes, they loll until the month of May
And then they jet back home again
(Crafty things)

Distressing letter to a duck

Dear Ida,

I sent Tom Cat a Christmas gift
Beribboned nice in Xmas lace,
A Portrait of three grinning Mice
To hang above his fireplace (snigger snigger)

Tom wouldn't speak to me for days!

Tom then sent me a birthday gift
Beribboned smart in cellophane
It was a jar of pickled eggs!!!

Dear Ida, you will know my rage!
Oh I'll never speak to Tom again!

From your friend Mother Hen

6

missmousemum@gmail.com

Email from Miss Mouse to her Mum

Hi Mum,
...I like those little Bats next door
I think they're fond of me
I think I'll make some currant buns
And ask them round for tea

I've seen those little Bats next door
A' swinging upside down
I think I'll hang some streamers up
So they can hang around

Come for tea

Oh, yes pleeease DO come

7

Mums reply...

...NO ...hang some streamers ACROSS , not UP !!
(tut tut)
Lace your ceiling dome
Then when they eat their currant buns
They'll really feel at home.
xxx

The Chocoholic Cat

A confession of 6 mice (snigger)

We took a piece of Chocolate
And wafted it about
Then we threw it in the Nettles
By the Chocoholic's house... tee hee

The greedy Cat emerged and ran
Into the Nettle field
Where, egged on by his
Pugging tooth,
He grabbed the Choccy piece

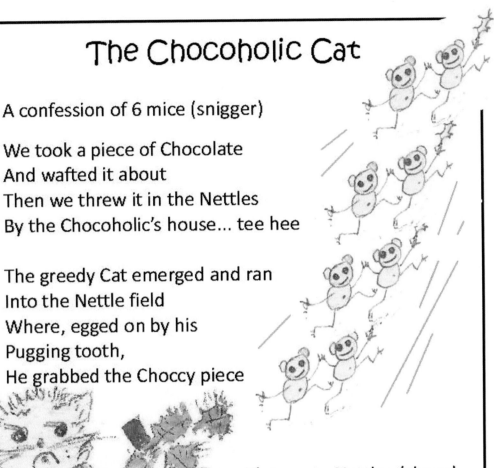

Along with twenty Nettles (sharp)
Oh! he cried and stung all day...
We watched him for ten minutes
Then went laughing on our way.

9

The Hedgehog and the Lobster

A very sporty Hedgehog...
.... a' spiked with bravery
Informed his prickly brothers
A wrestler he would be

Oh, that poor deluded Hedgehog!
His dream went sadly wrong
His spikes were too off putting...
And he had no takers on

Until a kindly Lobster,
On hearing of his plight,
(And quite immune to bristly backs)
Offered him a fight

Yes, offered him a fight lad
Oh! The Hedgehog spiked with glee
Now these two wrestle once a week
A sharp and cracking sight to see

10

The Greedy Cat

One Christmas Eve a greedy Cat
Sat down to write his Christmas List
And checked it twice to make quite sure
No item he required was missed

The list was eighteen pages long !!!
But still he wasn't satisfied
He left a note "Dear Santa Claus..
..the above all five times multiplied"!!!

11

When Santa came and read that list,
(all greedy children please take heed!)
He told his reindeer to ride on,
And left Tom nothing for his greed

12

A Cat's Dilemma

DEAR LITTLE READER
I am so relieved to see you!
Oh I've been stuck here all night!
Please go alert my mother of my plight...
(please, pleeeeease)

I've been as careless as can be,
I trod in wet cement you see
And now I'm in a fix....
Stuck all night... in a fright
Well, I was ok... 'til half past three...
But then the pesky mice discovered me...

....STUCK ALL NIGHT, TEE HEE

The Secret...

...have you ever seen a gardener
As good as Mistress Mouse?
Her flowers are growing
Taller than her house!

She waters and she feeds them,
She keeps the weeds at bay
and she has a little secret
which she told to me one day...

She gently whispered in my ear...
"I always sing to them, my dear"

15

The Violinist

Three cats sat chatting one dark night
When, much to their surprise,
A sound arose so sweet and pure...
...indeed it brought tears to their eyes!

They wallowed in sweet sorrow,
Their tears flowing over their chin,
When round the corner slid a mouse
Playing an old violin...

They applauded!, gave him silver!
Fast begged for more ......but he
Melted, (sharpish), into the night
And turned off his hidden C.D

snigger

16

The Kind Dentist

Look at the happy, thumping,
dancing Mad March Hare
I've seen him twizzling,
zipping, whizzing in the air

I've seen him bash his gnashers
in frenzied leaps of grace
So I'm making him a gum shield
to keep the pair in place

17

A Hint to all Flagging Comedians...

...LOOK

If you find that your jokes are a' flagging
As you work the Variety Halls...

...hire two laughing Hyenas
To sit in the Orchestra Stalls

BOOM
BOOM

A Tale From The Washing

On any Monday morning,
when the weather's fine
And the rain decides to take a day of rest

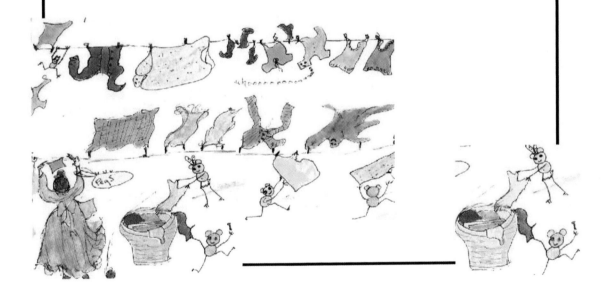

Yes, any Monday morning,
when wind and sun combine
We come out and do the thing we love the best...
...line dancing

Yes, we all hang out together
In zippy, madcap weather
LINE DANCING...Yahooooooo

Sheets Snapping
Shirts Zapping
Socks Swinging
Dresses Flinging
All are prancing
Line Dancing
Yahooooooooo

Llanfairpwllgwyngyllgogerychwyrndrobwillllantysiliogogogoch...

...tis the longest word in the dictionary
Eight and fifty letters long!!!
But I say with pride
When I was small
My mother knew a longer one

She'd stand and look me in the eye
And say that wondrous word to me
With a teacher look
Upon her face
In a voice that made me laugh with glee

I loved the sound but the gist of it
Passed like water o'er my head
Sometimes I thought it was my name...
...that super duper word she said.....

A Family Tree

Two mice asked of a learned cat
To help research their family tree
Could he trace their ancient roots?
He said he'd trace them (for a fee)

Next day he told the startled mice
"I've traced your roots, they lead...
...to the film star MICKEY MOUSE'!!!!!
And smiled, with tongue in cheek

"Your great grandpa was MICKEY MOUSE"!!!!!!
Oh! the two mice swelled with pride!
They danced with joy... and the lying cat
Laughed loud until he cried

23

The Grateful Host

A very kind
and thoughtful Tick
Lives on wild berries and toast

Not so much
a vegan as...
...not wanting to steal from its Host

The v. relieved
and grateful Host,
Amazed at this mannerly act...

Thank you, tick!

...applauded the Tick
on its thoughtfulness
And allows it to chill on his back

BERRY DISH

Revenge

A cheeky young squirrel was taunting a cat
Calling him spotty, you know, things like that
Saying the cat
Was a skunk in disguise
And showing him up
In front of the mice
The cat was offended, he upped sticks and went
But before he left home a letter he sent....

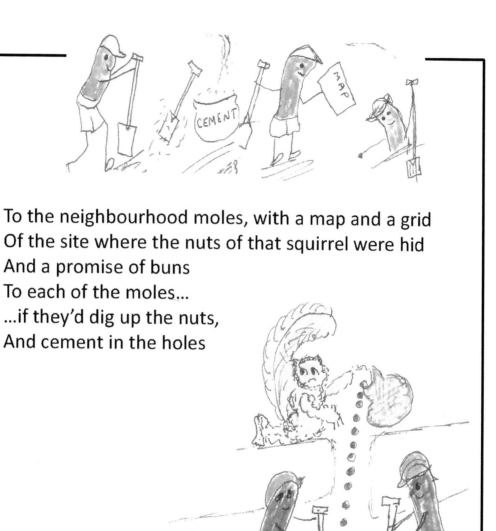

To the neighbourhood moles, with a map and a grid
Of the site where the nuts of that squirrel were hid
And a promise of buns
To each of the moles...
...if they'd dig up the nuts,
And cement in the holes

Whisper, Whisper

Miss Molly Cat is oh so kind,
in fact she's almost perfect!
But there's one thing I have to tell
She cannot keep a secret !

Fancy that ...a cat who cannot keep a secret
Oh Miss Molly don't you know it's wrong
To hear a secret then tell everyone?

Miss Molly Cat is oh so sweet, O, she is almost perfect!
But I'm afraid she has no friends
'cos she tells all their secrets

A Judgement

"I am charging this pair, A.Mouse and A.Cat
Of faking a fraudful Ventriloquist Act,
A.Mouse is charged with fooling the throng
By pretending to be a ventriloquist Doll

A.Cat will be jailed for he told everyone
He was throwing his voice, but keeping dumb!
They've conned lots of folk all over town...
A fraudulent pair, now take them both down

Smilers

There is something I have noticed...
...and I'm sure you've noticed too,
We all know someone don't we
Who, no matter what they do
They make us laugh!
Isn't it true?

look
at
mick →→

Even when they're being naughty OOPS
You just HAVE to laugh

29

Like, a cheeky little Spider dancing on a cat
And a naughty little Caterpillar
In his mothers hat
All kinds of things like that
Yes, we all know someone just like this

I really wonder why it is?
Are you one of them? ....Really ?
LUCKY YOU xx

NUTS

What if and just supposing...
...when nuts fall from the trees
What if and just supposing
They hurt their hand and knees,
It's such a long, long way to fall
I wouldn't be surprised at all

What if and just supposing
a secret spell was found...

...to magic them with parachutes...
to glide them safely down?

The Cheeky Sunflowers

Dear dotted, spotted Ladybirds
Come here, come here do
We know a clicking clacking game
We'd like to share with you

It involves you spreading out your wings
 And lining up in rows
Then being pushed about a bit
In a game called Dominoes

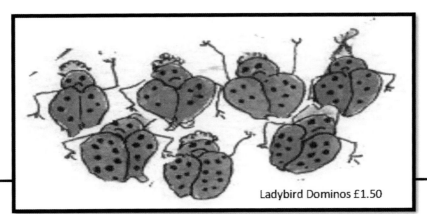

Ladybird Dominos £1.50

33

Oh! The Ladybirds cried
"Hey! no way!"
Go find another game to play
No!..
And, closing wings, they ran away.

Cheek!

34

A Little Old Lady's Lodgers

A Spider and one or two others,
Two blue eyed Bugs and a Flea
...ten Ticks and a Mouse
All dwell in my house
But they are no bother to me

The Spider and one or two others
Curtain my windows (for free)
The two blue eyed Bugs
Clear the crumbs from my rugs
And the Mouse shares my afternoon tea

The Flea and the Ticks keep my bed warm
(A big help, you have to agree!)
Aye, they dwell in my house
This mixed motley crowd
And they are a comfort to me.

36

Oven Scones

A little Mouse was running home...
...he ran because his mam
Was making him an oven scone
With cream and damson jam! Yummy

Five little Spiders wondered why
The little Mouse ran so
They decided to a' follow him
To see where he would go

Six little Rabbits sitting by
Saw the Spiders run
And decided to a' follow them
And join in all the fun

A little baking Mother Mouse,
As busy as a bee,
Saw this little running group
And asked them in for tea

She'd only made one oven scone
And needed, well, a score
So she put her little oven on
And baked eleven more.

awww

Goose Pimples

Goose pimples, Goose Pimples , Goose Pimples repose...

...from the tops of our heads ....to the tips of our toes.

And why ARE Goose Pimples residing on us?

Well to tell you the truth... we have just seen a GHOST!!!

39

Yes, we just saw a Ghost go a'twizzling round...

...with its arms in the air and its feet off the ground

It paused when it saw us, and winked a black eye

And that's why Goose pimples upon us abound

40

2 Ponderings from Dot Duck

I wonder why a smiling face...
goes into reverse
when someone looks it in the eye

And begs a penny from its purse????

Also... that Educated Squirrel, taught to use his head
Continues to hide nuts in holes!!!
Why won't he bottle them instead???

The Gnats' Concern...

"Oh friendly Frogs, our friendly Frogs,
Why do you leap so high?"
"Dear Gnats we are not leaping...
...we're trying hard to fly".

"Oh friendly Frogs, our friendly Frogs,
Please try some other day
For who will guard the lily pond
If you should fly away?"

Shell Songs

Sometimes we burst out singing, for no apparent cause
Sometimes we whistle little tunes, why?...nobody knows
Well, there HAS to be a reason for every single thing,
                LOOK...
...I once heard of a magic Elf ...
(I don't know if it's true my dear)
I'm told he carries songs in shells,
To blow into a listening ear...of a happy child!
Invisibly too! Could be you...
Well, perhaps that could be the reason we sing out
What do YOU think?

43

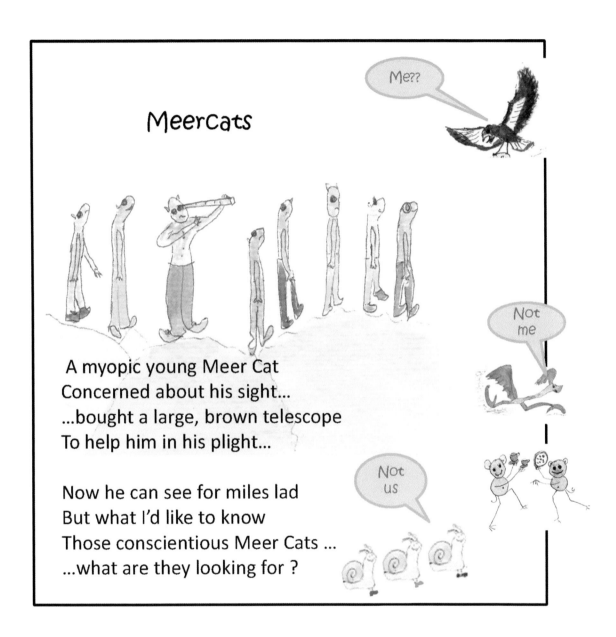

Meercats

A myopic young Meer Cat
Concerned about his sight...
...bought a large, brown telescope
To help him in his plight...

Now he can see for miles lad
But what I'd like to know
Those conscientious Meer Cats ...
...what are they looking for ?

44

The Wild Eyed Cat

Someone asked a wild eyed Cat
Why his eyes were thus
And why he sentries round his yard
Each night to dawn from dusk

'The answer is a Free Range hen',
The wild eyed Cat replied,
'She nightly sneaks into my yard
And ranges free inside...

She scrats among my prizey beans
(Of which she gives no hoot)
And that is why I sentry round
And wear this wild eyed look'.

45

The Inn Keeper's Dilemma

Thirteen peaceful sleeping Cats...
I'm loath to wake them but
The Mice are all a' signalling
And something is afoot

The Mice are all a' gathering
In groups of five or six
Tiptoeing and sniggering
Oh! Something is amiss

Thirteen peaceful sleeping guests
I'd love to leave them so... zzzz
But... the Mice are up to mischief
And the Cats will need to know

46

Snap!

Tom and Mick were playing cards,
The game was SNAP, (you know it)
T'was Mick's turn next to lay a card
But he simply would not show it

He stretched his arm a dozen times
And each time drew it back
Oh! Tom sat there on tenterhooks
Longing to shout SNAP!

47

But no...
scared Mick just wouldn't throw
Although his turn was due....
His heart was in his mouth 'cos he
Was choking on the word 'SNAP' too.

This impasse hung, 'til finally
Toms nerves snapped like thread,...
...he threw his cards down with a scream!
And Mick yelled 'SNAP' ...then fled.

48

Eiderdown Farm

Come and meet Miss Eider Duck
She sells her wares twice monthly
Soft pillows stuffed with Eiderdown
So soft and deep and plumpty

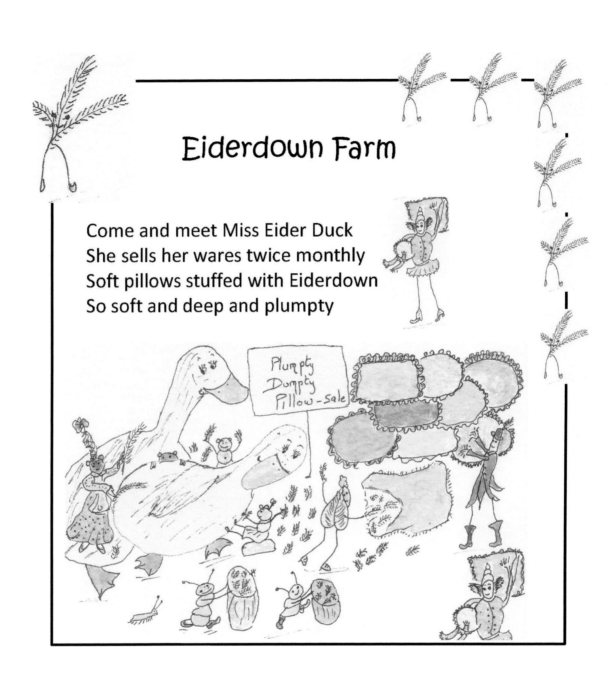

49

Visit all her feathered friends
They'll be so pleased to meet you
They'll let you test their Feathery nest
And for a penny, sell you.......
Soft and Plumpty, Deep and Comfy
Warm and Cosy, Clean and Rosy, gentle slumber Pillows

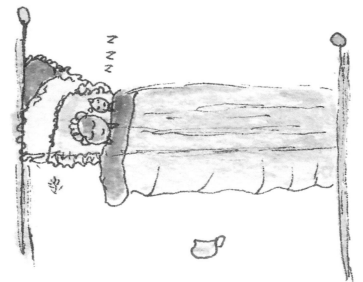

50

Boo!

Tell me, tell me, if you know
Why do we love Ghost stories so?
We shiver in delicious fright
When hearing spooky tales at night
Isn't that right?

51

And tell me, tell me if you can
Why we all talk of the Bogey Man...
...We know these tales cannot be true
But still we all like listening to....

...Spooky Wooky stories

BOO!

The Strange Case of a Chamois Leather

A "shammy deer" came to my house
Enquiring of his sister
He hadn't seen her for a while
And he really, really missed her

I shed a tear and told him 'why,
that very morn I'd seen her,
 a' working WITHOUT WAGES!!!
For the local Window Cleaner' !!!

53

To my surprise the "shammy" laughed
"Why, she's found her true vocation"
He thanked me, and went on his way!!.
A very puzzling conversation!

What's a chamois leather, then?

Why Sloths appear slow

A deep thinking Sloth,
Yes there are one or two,
Was lolling about the way those Sloth's do
Lolling about and letting his mind
Ponder on Einstein's Theory of Time

And as he was musing on Time versus Space
An enlightening look came over his face...

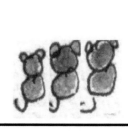

"WOW!! Eons ago we were already HERE !!
And we've had to hang on......in a slow second gear!

Crikey! we've had to slow down until humans
appeared!!

See ...

$$t = d \div s$$
$$d = s \times t$$
$$s = d \div t$$

......makes that clear!!!!!"

Wishing Well

Please don't be cross with our Wishing Well
If your wishes don't come true...
He's very old and deaf you see...
And an hearing aid is overdue

58

Dear Woodpecker

Oh I am not a snitch but I think you should know
Where the results of your peck peckings go

If you look through the trees
You will see a sly cat
With a shovel to hand
And a sack on his back

No matter the weather, he's there every day
To shovel your peckings, and steal them away

59

Yes he steals all your sawdust
To sell it, of course,
to the Travelling Circus...
...to strew on their floors !

60

38798497R00037

Printed in Poland
by Amazon Fulfillment
Poland Sp. z o.o., Wrocław